Zahn

Thousands of Bob Zahn cartoons have been published in all the
leading publications including The Wall Street Journal, Good
Housekeeping, Playboy, Woman's World, National Lampoon,
Better Homes & Gardens, National Enquirer, First and countless
other magazines worldwide.

ARI BERK

LOREN LONG

SCHOLASTIC INC.

ISBN 978-0-545-75179-7

Text copyright © 2012 by Ari Berk. Illustrations copyright © 2012 by Loren Long.
All rights reserved. Published by Scholastic Inc, 557 Broadway, New York, NY 10012, by arrangement with Simon & Schuster Books for Young Readers, an imprint of Simon & Schuster Children's Publishing Division. SCHOLASTIC and associated logos are trademarks and/or registered trademarks of Scholastic Inc.

12 11 10 9 8 7 6 5 4 3 2 1   14 15 16 17 18 19/0

Printed in the USA   08

This edition first printing September 2014

Book design by Dan Potash

The text for this book is set in Caslon Manuscript.

The illustrations for this book are rendered in acrylic and graphite.

For my mother and my son
—A. B.

To my father
—L. L.

The sun had set, and the shadows clinging to the walls of the cave began to wake and whisper.

"Chiro? Little Wing?" the bat-mother said to her child. "Tonight you must fly out into the world, and I will wait here for you."

"But the night is dark, Momma . . . darker than the moth's dark eyes . . . darker even than the water before dawn," the little bat exclaimed, twitching his ears this way and that.

"I know," whispered his mother.

"And when it is that dark outside, I cannot always see," Chiro admitted, stretching his wings.

"There are other ways to see," she told him, "other ways to help you make your way in the world."

"How?"

"Use your good sense."

"What is sense?" the little bat asked.

His mother folded him in her wings and whispered into his waiting ears, *"Sense is the song you sing out into the world, and the song the world sings back to you. Sing, and the world will answer. That is how you'll see.*

"Now fly from our cave to the pond where we bats like best to eat. Have your breakfast, then fly home, but do not go farther than the pond, not unless your song is sure."

And then she let him go.

Chiro fell into the cold air for an instant, then flapped and turned and flew out past the mouth of the cave and into the waiting night.

At first Chiro tried to peer his way through the dark. Long arms rose up in front of him, waving slowly, blocking his path. He could not see around them, or over them. Chiro was frightened.

But he remembered his mother's bright words:

"Use your good sense."

Chiro began to sing. Softly at first . . . .

. . . but then more surely. His song flew ahead of him, and soon he could hear something singing back.

Tall trees called out to him, chanted the lengths of their long branches and the girths of their rough trunks. Gleefully, he flew through the woods, past pines, over maples, and away.

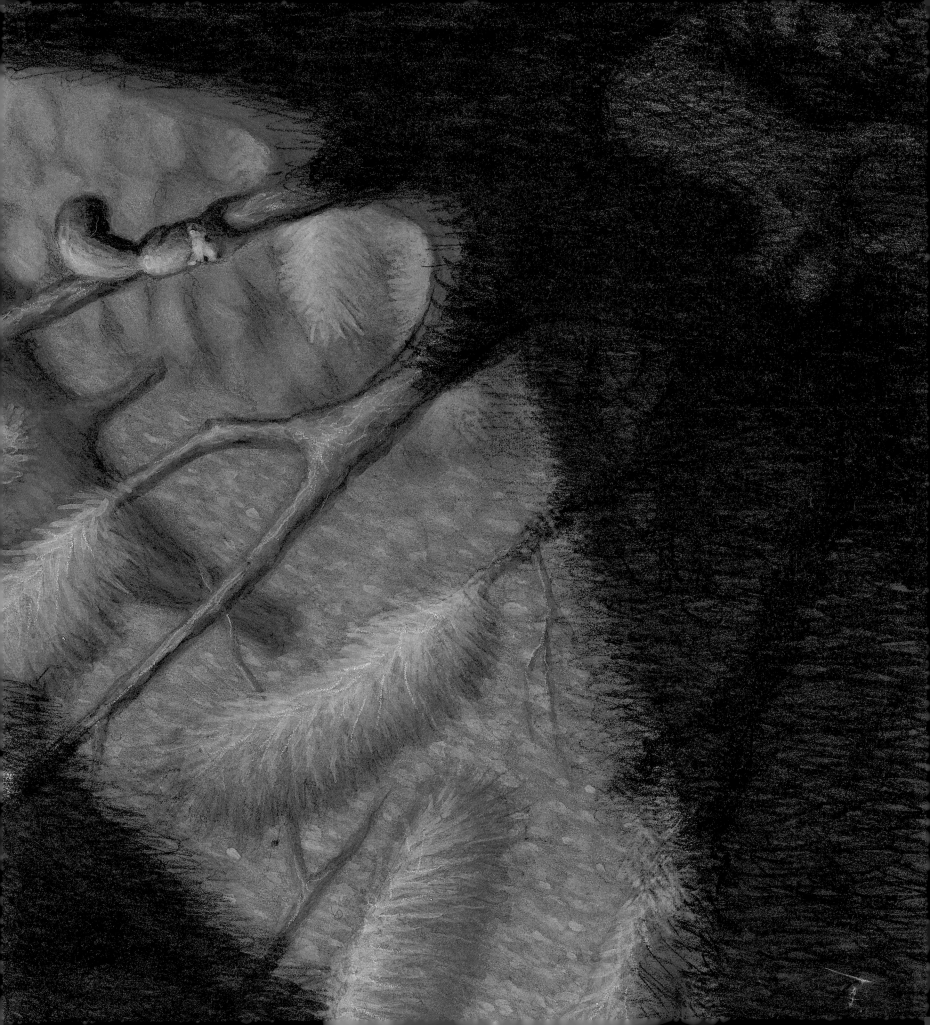

Flying higher now, Chiro saw something sliding through the sky toward him.

So out went his song, and where danger once threatened, now Chiro saw only a flock of friends flying above him on their evening errands.

As he flew farther, Chiro heard strange sounds: lines of noise, a thousand voices buzzing from one end of the sky to the other. For just a moment, Chiro didn't know what to do or which way to go.

But he followed his own song. In the sky behind him flowed a river of whispers, fading away. The pond was just ahead.

When Chiro came to the pond, singing still, he was very hungry. All the night creatures were there above the reeds, thousands of tiny, flying tasty things, each one humming a different tune. For Chiro each of their songs sounded like breakfast.

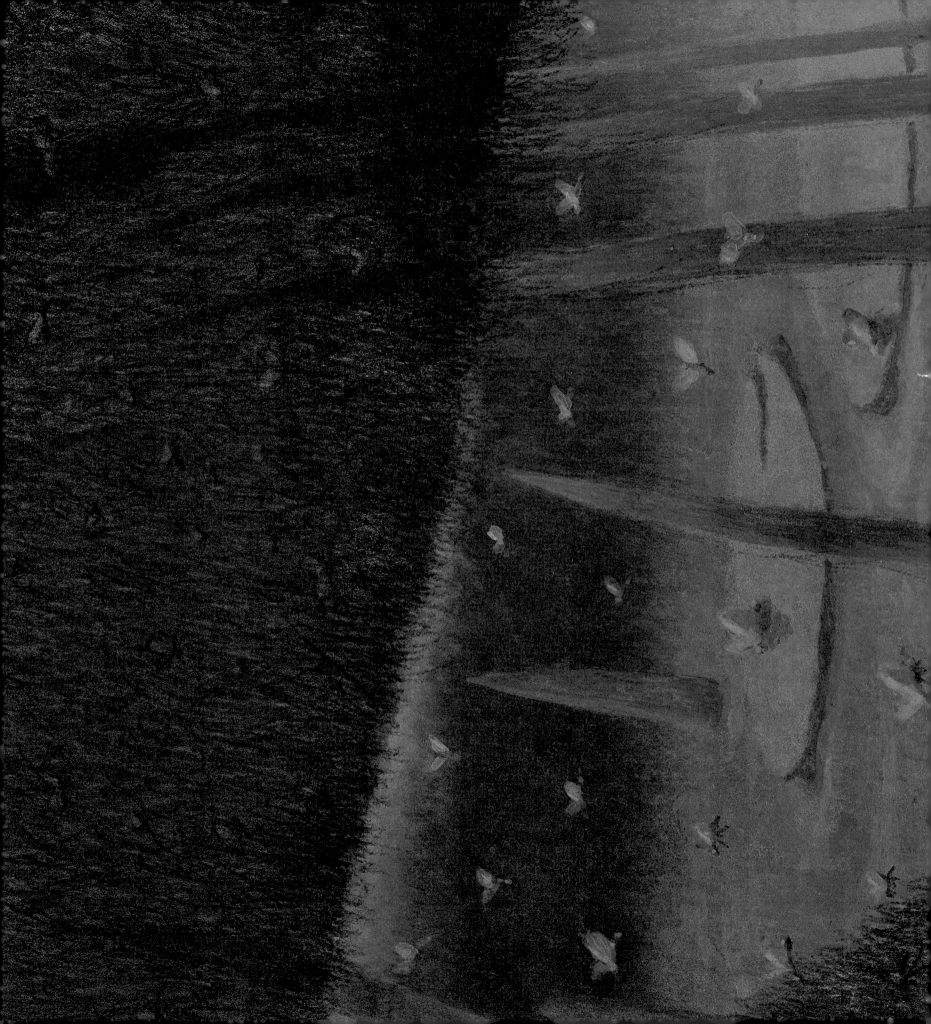

Chiro ate well that night.

When he was full, he stretched his wings again and thought about flying home, but he began to wonder, just a little. What lay beyond the pond? What lay beyond his mother's words?

So Chiro flew a bit farther and the familiar fell away from him. Out, out to the margins of the world. Then he was truly on his own.

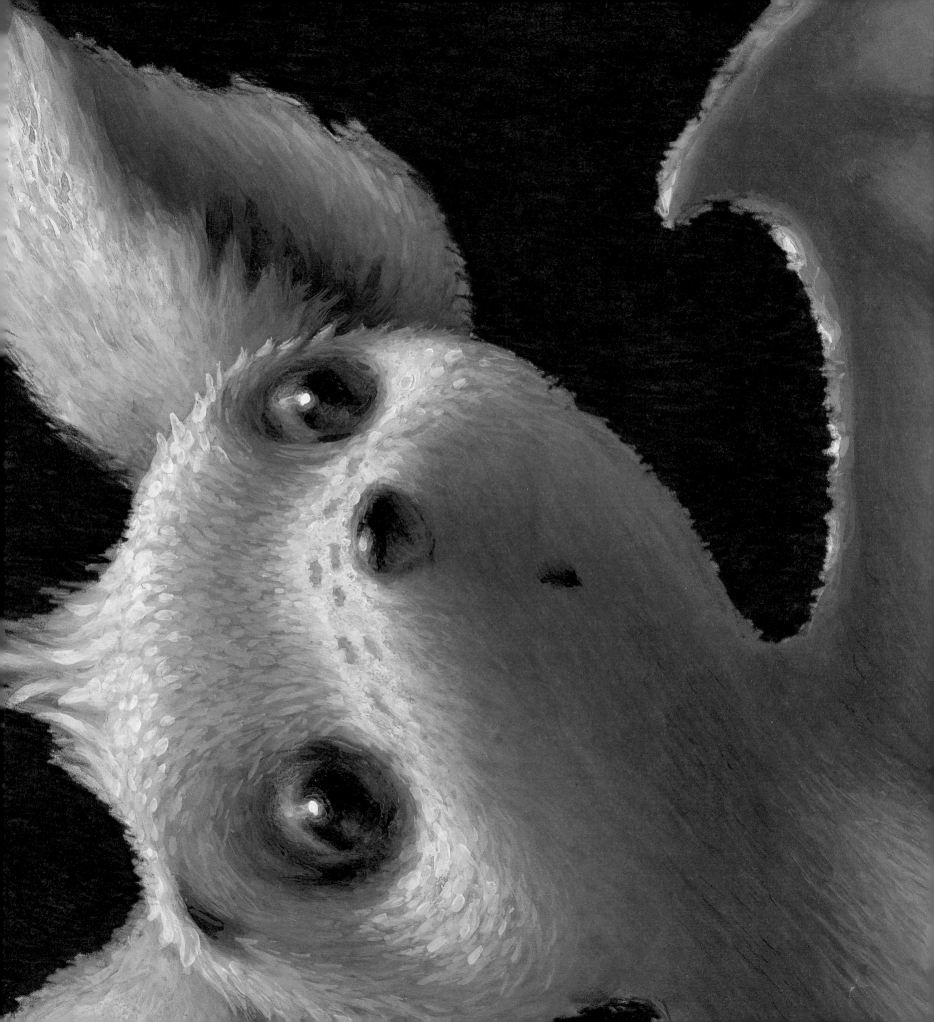

He flew fast toward a high dune, each grain of sand calling out in chorus as he passed. Chiro flapped up and over the top of the dune and out over the strand, singing louder than he ever sang before.

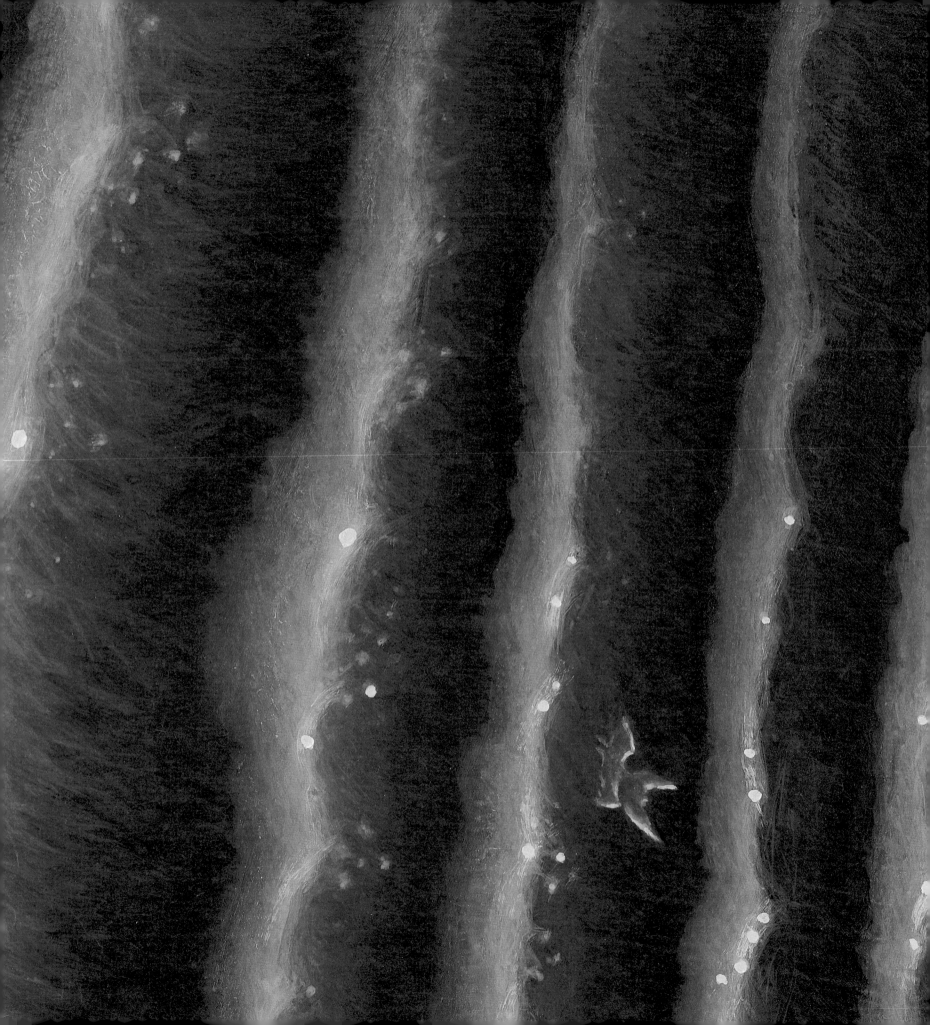

Out went his song over dark water then, again and again, each wave on the ocean rising up to greet him, each splash of sea foam becoming kin to him.

The sky began to change, grow light, and cast long shadows over the shore. With the morning came memory: his mother's voice, her warm wings. Chiro knew it was time to go home.

Flying higher than he'd ever flown, Chiro began to sing,
listening, listening . . .

The music of the land rose up in all of its many textures,
each tree, each cliff, each place he'd passed, until finally
the song of home added its voice to the others.

His cave called out from the blanketing shrubs and pillows of moss at its mouth, and Chiro followed that familiar sound back into the sheltering earth.

His mother caught him all up in her wings and asked, "Was it very dark in the world, Little Wing? What did you see?"

"Why, Momma!" Chiro said laughing, "It was very, VERY dark . . . ."

... and I saw everything!"

And then he yawned and turned his head into the warmth of her body, letting the rising sun's quiet song carry him, lull him, sing him to sleep.

The name Chiro (*cheer-o*) was inspired by the word "chiroptera," (from Greek, *cheir,* "hand" and *pteron,* "wing"), the order name for bats, the only mammals capable of true flight.

Ari Berk is the author of *The Secret History of Giants, William Shakespeare: His Life and Times,* and many other books for children and adults, including *The Runes of Elfland* (with artist Brian Froud), *The Secret History of Hobgoblins,* and most recently, *Death Watch* (Book One of the Undertaken Trilogy). When not writing, he moonlights as a professor of mythology and folklore. He lives in Michigan with his wife and son.

Visit him at ariberk.com.

Loren Long illustrated the newest version of *The Little Engine That Could* and, most recently, President Barack Obama's *Of Thee I Sing*. He also illustrated Frank McCourt's *Angela and the Baby Jesus*, wrote and illustrated *Otis*, and is part of the Design Garage for Jon Scieszka's Trucktown series. Loren's work has appeared in *Time*, *Sports Illustrated*, *Forbes*, the *Wall Street Journal*, and the *Atlantic*. He lives in Ohio with his wife and two sons.